MW00986183

THEY CALL ME
NO SAM!
by NO SAM!

As Dictated to
DREW DAYWALT
Illustrated by Mike Lowery and **NO SAM!**

Clarion Books
An Imprint of HarperCollins*Publishers*

Clarion Books is an imprint of HarperCollins Publishers.

Library of Congress Control Number: 2023943607
ISBN 978-0-35-861290-2

The artist used Procreate, Photoshop, and a pencil to create
the digital illustrations for this book.
Typography by Sarah Nichole Kaufman and Julia Feingold
24 25 26 27 28 LBC 7 6 5 4 3

First Edition

To Reese, who always reads my stuff
—Drew Daywalt

To Abigail for picking me out and
taking me home.
Thanks for believing in me.
—Sam Daywalt

For Professor Avery Sharpe
–Mike Lowery

DAY 1

DEAR DIARY,

I feel like I should introduce myself, since this is my first diary entry ever.

My name is **NO SAM!** and I am a human being.

Here's me.

HUMAN Being ↓

1

That's not the name I was born with, though. My real name is Grrowlo-Ruff-Ruff. But since that name was apparently unpronounceable to Mike, the naked-monkey-thing I used to live with, I've had to settle for the name he gave me: **NO SAM!**

And here's Mike.

mike

Mike is one hundred ninety-six years old, but in naked-monkey-thing years that's only twenty-eight. I *think*. You'll have to check my math.

Most of the time Mike wasn't even around. He left early in the morning and came home super late at night. So while my days were a little lonely, it wasn't so bad. I mean, he left the TV on, so at least I was able to watch the news.

Mike never took me outside for a walk, and that's okay. After watching the news, I could see why. It was a dangerous world out there, filled with pirates and monsters and killer robots. At night, after he came home from work, Mike would take a shower and then go out again, and I would just watch more news.

I began to wonder why Mike even wanted a human being like me around. Since the dawn of time, you see, human beings and naked-monkey-things have had an unspoken contract that defines why we live and work together as a team. Human beings like myself have taken on the role of defender of the home. All in all, we have a lot going for us as a species.

Poor, dim-witted naked-monkey-things, on the other hand, have no fur to stay warm, no claws, dull teeth, no sense of smell, lousy hearing, and only two legs for running. Pitiful, really. But the one advantage they *do* have, that we human beings do not, is . . .

5

SAM'S SUPER AMAZING awesome SURVIVAL attriBUTes

Sharp teeth

SUPERIOR intelligence

warm fur

EEEEE

TerrifYinG DEAth scream

SHARP claws

incrediBle speeD

HUMAN Being

Hands.

Which makes them better at three very important things: petting, scratching behind ears, and opening bags of food.

And while Mike was fine at opening the food bag most of the time, he never really lived up to his part in the "petting and scratching" department. And that just didn't make sense to me.

But then again, a lot of things about Mike didn't make sense. For instance, on his birthday I offered to share my favorite chew toy with him.

Mike didn't like the present. It was then that I realized that Mike and I weren't right for each other. So I ran away.

And that's how I ended up in prison.

But you know what? Prison's not so bad. Not compared to Mike, anyway. He always smelled like anger and frustration, and I don't know if you've ever smelled those two things, but they're terrible. Kind of like rotten fish dipped in stinky mayo and hot sauce.

All the guards are naked-monkey-things. I've tried asking them how long until I get out, but they don't seem to understand what I'm even saying.

I think she meant to comfort me, but just the thought of Mike showing up to take me back sent shudders down my spine. Going back to live with him would be the worst thing that could possibly happen.

As I was settling in for bed tonight, one of the guards came by and gave me an ominous warning . . .

Her words haunted me. First of all, what in the world is a *pug*? And *"take me out"*? I've seen enough TV to know what *that* means.

It means **NINJA ASSASSINS!**

DAY 2

DEAR DIARY,

Today two strangers came to visit me. At first I was worried that they were going to "take me out," but it quickly became evident that these two weren't ninjas. Instead, they were a pair of naked-monkey-things named Gary and Elaine. They were very friendly, but they reeked of anxiety and concern and even a little guilt about something. What it was, I had no clue. My sense of smell is good, but not *that* good.

They spent a long time petting me and talking, but they never talked *to me*. As a matter of fact, they spent the whole time talking to each other, even though they were looking at me. Talk about awkward!

"Isn't he cute?" said Elaine. "I think Justin would just love this little guy."

"He is cute," Gary said, "but I wonder if he's trained."

"Either way, Justin needs a friend right now. Moving has been hard on him. And all that time we spend in the lab . . ."

Gary nodded. "Let's bring him by tomorrow. If they click, then we'll take Mr. Fuzzy Pants here home with us."

Mr. Fuzzy Pants? That's a new one. But as far as I'm concerned, he can call me whatever he wants if he springs me from prison and gives me a new home to defend.

But what was that "click" Gary mentioned? They want me to click with this Justin? A strange request. But if clicking is what they want, then clicking is what they'll get.

I'm gonna have a hard time sleeping tonight, but that's okay. I need to practice my clicking anyway.

DAY 3

DEAR DIARY,

Gary and Elaine brought their offspring, Justin, with them today. I think he's about eighty-four years old, which makes him twelve or so in naked-monkey-thing years. The poor kid smelled lonely. Funny thing about naked-monkey-things: they can't smell emotions. It's just one of the many reasons they need human beings like me to help take care of them.

As soon as I saw them, I started clicking. I must not be very good at it, because they all laughed.

And then Justin did it. He clicked back at me!

I clicked again. We were clicking!

Next, Justin did something that no one has ever done to me. He started petting me . . . *behind the ears*. Mike never petted me at all, let alone behind the ears. I knew that on the few occasions when I'd managed to get a paw back there and scratch, it felt great, but this . . . **ZOWIE!**

What an amazing, wonderful, delightful sensation! I'm embarrassed to say that it made me do something I've never done before. I started licking and kissing Justin, the nicest person I'd ever met!

"Looks like they're clicking to me," said Gary.

After that, they took me out to the guard at the front desk. I'm not sure what happened, but I saw them give the guard money and sign a piece of paper, and then we walked out.

Nothing but a bribe to a prison guard and I was free! And I still didn't even know what I had been accused of doing in the first place.

When we got to their home, Justin's parents made him put a leash on my collar before we left the car. Probably so Justin wouldn't run off and get into trouble.

What an amazing house! I could smell a cat

living in here somewhere: male, a young adult. I could also tell he was lazy, pre-diabetic, and looking for meaning in his life.

As we walked up the front walkway, it occurred to me that we had made it all the way home without being attacked by any of the monsters or aliens or bandits that I'd seen on the news. It was sheer luck that we made it here alive at all. I suddenly felt ashamed. How could I have let my guard down so quickly? But these poor defenseless naked-monkey-things will never have to worry about their safety again. **NO SAM!** is on the job!

If I do a good job, they'll need me around. And if they need me around, they'll never take me back to prison. And if they don't take me back to prison, Mike can never show up there and take me back. Yes, this family is my ticket to happiness!

When they opened the front door, I ran inside and almost fainted with joy. Right there was the most beautiful *pooping rug* I'd ever seen. I didn't want to insult my new hosts, so I marched in and showed them how grateful I was.

They weren't very appreciative of my gesture, but they did know my name already, which was nice.

Justin led me upstairs to his room and let me sleep in his bed with him. I'd never slept in a naked-monkey-thing bed before and it was just as dreamy as I had hoped. Naked-monkey-things are like big, bed-warming hot water bottles. Who knew?

I am adding this bed-warming function to the list of primary naked-monkey-thing life skills.

In review of the day, I couldn't be happier. And I know Justin feels the same, because that lonely feeling I've been smelling on him has diminished significantly.

I've decided it is my mission to make it go away entirely.

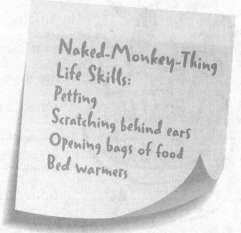

Naked-Monkey-Thing
Life Skills:
Petting
Scratching behind ears
Opening bags of food
Bed warmers

DAY 4

DEAR DIARY,

I woke up early and realized I was incredibly thirsty. Luckily, the Petersons have a beautiful drinking room with a large, ornate fountain.

Next I trotted into the eating room, where Justin was dining alone. He smelled a little lonely still, but it made me feel nice that the smell diminished again when he saw me.

I was distracted by a delicious smell coming from under the sink. I nosed open

drinking fountain

a little door and inside was a white treasure chest filled with what smelled like the most fantastic food I'd ever inhaled.

"No, Sam! That's garbage!" Justin said, pulling me away. "You know what you want?"

Yeah. Garbage, apparently, I thought.

"You want SCRATCHIES!"

I do? What's scratchies?

Justin rushed over and started scratching my neck and behind my ears. Was this SCRATCH-IES??! Because it was sensational, marvelous, magnificent! In fact, words completely fail to describe the ecstasy of scratchies! They fall and clatter like broken pottery, ineffective in any way at describing the absolute joy brought on by scratchies. It was like he pressed magic buttons on my neck that caused my tongue to shoot out and start licking and kissing him!

"You want some scratchies, buddy?" he asked. "Huh? Do ya?"

Good heavens. **YES SIR, I DO WANT SCRATCHIES!!**

"Who wants some SCRATCHIES?!"

I just said me! I thought we just established who wanted them!

"You're the best, Sam. I love you."

Weird. He forgot to say the "NO" part of my name. Poor guy. His memory is terrible. But either way, I love him too. Twenty-four hours in and I love him.

Then Justin hopped over to the other side of the room and pointed at a pair of bowls on the floor.

"Here, buddy! We got you your own food and water bowls," he said. Then Justin poured out some "human being chow" for me. I was curious as to why they'd gotten a little bowl of water for me, since they already had a drinking room with a big white fountain.

NOTE TO SELF:
Obtain mirrors to see where these buttons are that trigger my leg to stick out and start kicking like that.

VERY ENTHUSIASTIC HUMAN BEING ↓

CHOW

Justin finished breakfast and started for the door with his backpack and books. "C'mon, Sam. Let's go outside."

And before I had a chance to use the pooping rug, Justin put the leash on me and led me outside to the front yard. He must have felt really insecure that he was going to run off, but as his protector, I was happy to make sure he didn't.

When we got there, he stopped and stared at me like it was my turn to do something. I just stared back at him.

"Go, Sam," he said. "C'mon, buddy. Go."

Ugh. Poor kid. I'm not Go Sam, I'm NO SAM!

"C'mon, buddy. Go," he repeated.

Go where? I thought. It was all so confusing! And to make matters worse, I had to poo so badly

I could barely stand still. But I most certainly was not going to poo outside on the ground like some kind of wild beast.

Thank goodness he eventually gave up on this Go game of his and got me back inside before I had an accident on the lawn. Just in time to use the rug.

NO, SAM! Why? I just took you outside!

Yeah, and you almost made me have an accident on the front lawn! (I thought it, but I didn't say it.)

After Justin cleaned up the rug, he looked out the window and got the most bizarre look on his face. I followed his gaze to see a girl naked-monkey-thing walking down the sidewalk. She looked to be about eighty years old, same as Justin. When I looked back from the girl to Justin, he still had that look in his eyes.

I've never seen anyone act like that in my entire life. And his lonely smell suddenly increased!

After she rounded the corner, he turned to me and said, "Wow, didja see that, Sam? She was wearing a *Plant Girl and Fire Boy* T-shirt! That's like my favorite comic book ever!"

I just listened. That's what friends do, after all. (Also, Plant Girl and Fire Boy sound like a great duo, if not a slightly dangerous combination.)

"Oh, Sam! All I want is someone to hang out with, and she seems perfect. But you saw the way she walked by. She didn't even see me. No one in this town even knows I'm alive."

First off, my name is **NO SAM!** Not Oh Sam.

He was getting closer, at least. And secondly, how could anyone not know he's alive? He's breathing, isn't he?

Before I could put any more thought into it, he gathered his books and shuffled out the door, all mopey and sullen. I admit it: I was worried. As his protector, I didn't like that his emotions were so tied to this other monkey-thing. And I especially didn't like not knowing why.

I still had a house to protect, and presumably Gary and Elaine to watch over. I followed their scent to a strange door.

I could smell Gary and Elaine on the other side. And they smelled like a mix of excitement, hope, and determination. Clearly they were safe, so I decided to get a better look at the rest of the house. If I was going to be head of security, I'd need to know what I was working with.

I smelled cat everywhere, but I saw no cat.

One nice thing about the eating room is the viewing platform they installed next to the window looking out over the side yard. This vantage point will prove useful if attacked from the west. There is a similar viewing platform in the pooping-rug room.

NOTE TO SELF:
Find out if cats can be invisible.

Next up, I noticed a mysterious closed door. Something inside stank of dust and plastic and had a slight tinge of burn-y smell. I put this on the list of possible threats.

In the back room there was a massive sliding glass door, which provided an ample view if we were attacked from the backyard. It was also in this room that I discovered the Petersons had installed both a chewing chair *and* a peeing couch for me! How thoughtful!

But best of all was the human being door that they'd installed at the bottom of their back door. They really did think of everything. I found that the door was a little snug, but with some work, I could get through it well enough.

Once outside, I took in the sights and smells.

I heard the most horrific tinkling music coming from the front of the house. I immediately searched the fenced perimeter of the yard for an emergency access tunnel. To my shock, there wasn't one! Yet the music was so terrifying that I knew I had to confront it immediately.

When I finally emerged, the music was gone. I missed whatever strange, ghostly abomination was lurking, but I will be ready next time!

Next thing that got my attention was the lady next door—who, by the way, has snakes for hair.

She looked innocent enough. *Too* innocent,

actually. But the snakes for hair . . . it reminded me of something, but I couldn't put my paw on what. I'd have to keep an eye on her.

Once I knew the outer perimeter of the house was safe, I made my way back inside just as Gary and Elaine emerged from the mysterious metal door.

They looked around and became angry for no reason whatsoever!

But if there's one thing I've learned about naked-monkey-things, it's that their moods can change in an instant. That's okay. My main concern is keeping them safe. Not only is it my duty as a human being, but keeping them safe means not being sent back to the shelter, and *not* being found by Mike. Despite my moody hosts, I already love it here.

Speaking of unpredictable behavior, almost immediately after yelling at me, I caught Gary doing something so sick, so ridiculously unsanitary, that you may not believe me. I went to get a drink of water in the drinking room and found Gary sitting on the big white water bowl.

"That's strange," I thought. Then, to my horror, I realized from the strained look on his face that he was **POOPING INTO OUR DRINKING WATER!** Didn't he know we had a perfectly good rug for that??

I started yelling at him to stop, explaining in no small detail that he was contaminating our drinking supply! But he just slammed the door in my face and yelled some gibberish at me. I think he was embarrassed to be caught doing something so awful.

(I used to suspect Mike of doing the same thing, but at least he was smart enough to close the door and hide his shameful habit. Gary, on the other hand, didn't even have the intelligence to do that. Luckily there's a little thingie-thing on the fountain that resets the water so it's clean enough to drink again, but still.)

I spent the rest of the day making my rounds, and by afternoon I could smell Justin coming home. When he entered, I couldn't help myself; I ran and jumped at him over and over. I have to say that one of the many evolutionary design flaws of naked-monkey-things is that their faces are too far from the ground. It makes them terribly hard to kiss.

Justin smelled hopeless again, and I caught him glancing out the window at the girl walking past. What had she done to him? Whatever it was, I didn't like it.

"Justin? Could you take Sam for a walk? He had an accident on the floor today," Elaine yelled from behind the metal door.

I didn't have an accident on the floor. I just peed on it, like you're supposed to.

"C'mon, Sam, let's go," Justin said.

I was getting the feeling he was never going to get my name right.

Just like this morning, Justin took me to the end of the grass and looked me in the eye. "Okay, Sam," he said. "Now, go."

Before I could ask him where, exactly, I was supposed to go, I spied two naked-monkey-things walking down the street. At first I bristled and growled. What if they were here to bring harm to Justin? But then they turned, smiled, and waved. My fears were allayed. If there's one thing I've learned from TV, it's that the good guys smile. And bad guys frown.

At dinnertime, everyone gathered in the eating room at the table. "How'd it go today?" Justin asked his parents as they began to eat.

"Well," said Gary, "he drank from the toilet, broke a lamp, chewed the chair, peed on the floor, then tracked mud in from the backyard, where he dug a huge hole under the fence, which I had to fill in. Otherwise, he was an angel."

"Oh," said Justin. "I meant with your experiments."

"Oh, that," said Gary. "Well, we're having trouble with some of the DNA sequences on the computer models, but that's to be expected. This is going to take time, that's all."

"About Sam, Justin," his mother continued.

Suddenly Justin smelled scared.

"He's got some behavioral issues we're going to have to address," she said. "It's not your fault. Or even his, really. He was just never trained. Do you think you could spend some time working with him?"

"Of course," Justin said.

Training? Really? I mean, I know I'm not a very experienced protector, but I've only been on the job for one day. And no offense to Justin, but what's *he* going to teach me?

But suddenly, I worried that they were

disappointed in me. What if they took me back to prison? I needed to turn this conversation around fast. Maybe if I clicked some more, that would help.

"Dad, look. He's doing that thing with his lips again."

Justin laughed at me and clicked back. Gary and Elaine laughed too.

Nailed it! Whew! Crisis averted. Tomorrow I will redouble my efforts.

DAY 5

DEAR DIARY,

After breakfast, Justin took me outside on another of his mystery walks. After what seemed like an interminable length of time, he finally brought me back inside. And thank goodness for that! As soon as I got back in, I used the pooping rug. It was really a close one.

"You can't keep doing this," Justin said as he cleaned up the rug. "You're supposed to poop out-side."

What?! First of all, that would be humiliating. I don't see *him and his parents* pooping in the front yard! And secondly, there's no rug outside. Where am I supposed to go, on the *grass?* Ludicrous!

Clearly his mind was confused, and as he looked out the front window, I knew why. The girl naked-monkey-thing was walking by, and Justin suddenly reeked of hope and sadness and loneliness. She was really messing with his mind. Before I could ponder it another second, Justin was out the door, a tornado of backpack, jacket, and flopping limbs.

Oh well. Time to get to work. I had a house to protect. After doing my rounds to all the viewing platforms, I could confirm that all was safe. But then I heard an absolutely horrid sound coming from Gary and Elaine's sleeping room!

I gave a perfunctory *woof* to gather my courage, then raced upstairs. And what I saw made my tail curl. There stood Elaine with a

BRAIN-MELTING HEAT CANNON!

Now, why they would keep something so dangerous in the house is beyond me. I've never seen any Popsicle monsters around here. (Don't laugh. I've seen them on TV.)

I know I'm here to protect the Petersons, but I never thought it would be *from themselves!* I immediately started yelling for her to drop the thing. But as I was trying to save her, she *aimed it at me!* Was she completely bananas?!

I had no choice but to retreat. After she left the room, though, I knew I had to take action before she melted her brain, or worse . . . *mine.*

After the unfortunate chapter with Elaine this morning, I decided to clear my head with a nice long patrol. I saw that Gary had indeed filled in my security access tunnel. The poor animal had no idea that I'd dug it for his own protection. Luckily, I quickly spotted a new location for a tunnel, this one hidden under a thick cluster of bushes.

Once liberated from the backyard, I took stock of the surrounding neighborhood. The woman with snakes for hair (I'll call her Lady Snakehair) was working in her garden next door. The two men in white jumpsuits were nowhere to be seen, but their vehicle was parked just up the street.

But the thing that was most strange was that there were these large treasure chests lining the street, one in front of each house.

The aroma wafting from them was delicious! I pushed one over to investigate, and my suspicions were quickly validated. They were indeed full of aromatic treasures!

Why would anyone put treasure out in their front yard? And not just the Petersons; the whole street had left chests full of delectable awesomeness out on the street!

Later in the day, I had just finished working on the chewing chair and was about to go on patrol again, when I heard the tinkling of a bell. At first I thought it was a fairy, but as I rounded the corner of the hall I found myself face-to-face with—

When I asked him his name, he told me it was *"Meow,"* and sadly, that seems to be the only word he knows.

Now, to be fair, I've never actually met a real cat before. I mean, I've seen them on TV at Mike's apartment, and they seemed great. All the ones on TV can talk and have magical powers. But this one? Not so much.

At any rate, he's nice enough, and he seems to like me because he follows me around, uttering his name over and over again. I've never considered myself much of a cat person, but I like Meow. I can tell he has a beautiful spirit, but his inability to talk is keeping it caged up inside. I'm hoping that with some time and a little patience, I'll be able to teach him to speak naked-monkey-thing-ese like the cats on TV.

A small note about Meow: after spending an entire day with him, I noticed the most peculiar thing. Meow never seems to go to the bathroom. I even showed him how to use the pooping rug and peeing couch, but he was entirely uninterested.

And in an equally astonishing miracle of science, Meow is able to make little snack treats in his *magic sand oven*. So clearly he *does* have magical powers. The naked-monkey-things don't like the treats at all, and Meow is indifferent to them, but I must admit, I find them irresistible, with a delicious crunchy outer shell.

DAY 6

DEAR DIARY,

Today began with Gary and Elaine yelling at me for "getting into all the trash cans on the street." Could they have been talking about the treasure chests? I started to worry that they weren't happy with the job I was doing, but then, to my astonishment, they awarded me with a fancy *medal of honor.*

So they seemed unhappy, but also quite pleased. I just don't get naked-monkey-things.

After breakfast with Justin, he did that annoying thing where he takes me outside *right* when I have to go to the bathroom. Will he never learn? As he and I were standing on the front lawn, who came by but that girl naked-monkey-thing. It was eerie. With just a smile, she filled Justin to the brim with a mix of longing and painful hope. The yard clouded up so much from his emotions that I could barely breathe.

After she left, he just looked at me and said, "Omigosh, Sam. She smiled at us?! Didja see that?"

I did, and I didn't like it one bit. I growled at her to let him know how I felt.

"C'mon, Sam. Chill OUT," he whispered. "I'm just trying to make a new friend. Her name is Phoebe."

Phoebe? Was I supposed to know who that is? Is she famous?

"And she plays *Magical Monsters*! How cool is that?"

Wait. What? She plays with magical monsters? That doesn't sound safe!

But Justin just hurried me into the house, then ran off with the most ridiculous look on his face, a pathetic cloud of giddy hope trailing behind him. It was like a spell had been cast on him.

A spell . . . wait a minute! I'd been a fool for not seeing it immediately. There was only one answer.

Think about it.

   1. She casts spells.

   2. She has some kind of magic cards (and
      apparently plays with magical monsters—
      not good).

   3. She's controlling his mind.

   4. She's smiling innocently the whole time.

And here's the clincher . . . she has a *cat!* I
smell it all over her every time she comes by.
Ladies and gentlemen of the jury, I rest my case:
this girl's an evil wizard!

I've seen it all on TV at Mike's. Some wizards have owls, some have bats, some have snakes, and some even have gargoyles! There was even one with a mean little baby dragon. But the worst ones have cats! This is a grave security threat indeed.

I decided to clear my head with a nice long patrol. Outside, I noticed Lady Snakehair standing defiantly in her front yard, arguing with some kind of muscled warrior guy.

I have a pretty strict policy in my life to not trust people with snakes for hair. There's just something unnerving about it.

The rest of the day was fairly uneventful, but there is one thing I should mention. After all the potential dangers around here, it's refreshing to report something positive. And it has to do with that van that's been parked on the street.

When I went over and smelled it, I could sense the two men from before. They reeked of anxiety and determination. Additionally, I smelled hoagies and pizza.

I decided to investigate. Scratching on the rear doors of the van immediately confirmed my suspicions.

Other than the food and the emotions of the two men, there was also a slightly burn-y, oily, plastic and electronics scent from all the computers and tech gear. I asked them what they were doing parking on the street every day.

They looked at me for a long time, then did the most incredible thing: they gave me my own hoagie! They called each other Drago and Grisha and spoke a dialect of naked-monkey-thing that I had never heard before. I didn't realize naked-monkey-things had more than one language.

By the time I left, I knew these guys were A-OK. I'm good with naked-monkey-things that way.

Later, in the evening, I decided that I would begin nightly patrols of the house. I'm glad I did, because I made an alarming discovery. Another evil entity is aligning against the Petersons.

I had just gotten a drink from the drinking

room and was making my way to the living room
when I glanced out the sliding glass doors to the
backyard. Just outside the window, I saw something that caused my blood to run cold. Staring
directly at me was what I can only describe as . . .
a Ghost Wolf.

There we were. Two warriors: myself, flesh and bone, and the Ghost Wolf, an eerie horror from some phantom realm. For the longest time, we just stared at each other, fire burning in our eyes as we began to growl. It was like this sickening minion of the dark could read my mind, could act in exactly the same way, at *exactly* the same moment that I did!

Then Meow approached and asked me what I was staring at.

I turned back to the Ghost Wolf and, to my total shock, there was Meow's translucent spirit, sitting next to him. It was as if the Ghost Wolf was mocking me, for he had clearly stolen Meow's soul and was holding it prisoner. I yelled for Meow to run. This battle was mine.

I had freed Meow's spirit from the grips of the Ghost Wolf! Then I charged, screaming, into battle. I was determined to send this demigorgon back to the very shadows of whatever hell he'd come from.

The battle raged for what seemed like an eternity, until it was interrupted . . . by Justin.

"No, Sam! Stop it!"

He pulled the blinds closed just as the Ghost
Wolf turned away. Just when I had the foul thing
on the run! Had he not seen its bristling fur, its
ferocious teeth, the fiery hatred in its eyes? Justin
hugged me and petted me. And slowly, as I calmed
down, I realized what had really happened, and
suddenly I felt the warmth of embarrassment.

Justin couldn't see ghosts. Clearly, this hell-hound was visible only to me. And this ability was a gift, but it was also a curse. For now, my only comfort was that at least I knew my foe. Even though I had driven him off, he would definitely return. Probably at night.

And be really scary.

DAY 7

DEAR DIARY,

This morning was rough. On the one hand, the Ghost Wolf seemed to be gone, but Gary and Elaine were especially tired and irritable.

Gary just stumbled past me in a daze, went into the lab, and closed the door behind him. Turns out the reason neither of them are ever at breakfast is because they work so late, then get up and start working again before Justin and I are even out of bed. Clearly, they're not getting enough sleep. And I'm really becoming concerned for Gary's safety. Working in that lab must be incredibly taxing on his insufficient, feeble little brain.

Justin was in a terrible mood this morning too, and I just don't understand why. Before he even came downstairs, I used the pooping rug so that later, when he took me outside, I could focus more closely on what, exactly, he wanted me to *do* out there.

But when he saw that I'd used the rug *for its*

intended purpose, he got angry with me. I think it has something to do with his constantly wavering emotions. It was that evil wizard, Phoebe. She was tampering with his feelings!

I had to find the source of Phoebe's wizard power, because it was undeniable. Justin was sick. He was more desperate than ever to spend time with her, and I could smell his yearning growing stronger every day. As I was contemplating how to best her, Justin grabbed his backpack and jacket and slumped out the door.

I watched him walk slowly to school. He seemed so sad. I mean, he had me, and that made his loneliness go away, but whenever he thought about her, he smelled like a different kind of lonely. I would have to best this evil wizard before she completely wrecked him.

I decided to calm my nerves by giving Meow his first language class. And while he wasn't able to make any new words yet, I was astounded at how attentive he was.

After language class, I took a nap, then worked on the chewing chair, followed by another nap. Naps are not to be underestimated. After a slow day at home, things picked up in a terrible way when I saw Justin walking home from school.

He stank of anxiety, mixed with a desperate

need to *do* something—although what, I did not know. Phoebe's dark wizard magic was really tearing him up, the poor kid.

But then, all of a sudden, he got this look on his face like he had made a decision. And his stink of nervousness went through the roof. So did his sense of determination.

Holy smokes, she was using her magic to pull him to her. Like metal to a magnet. Like a moth to a flame.

Oh **NO!** Moths who fly into flames die! I knew I had to act.

I blasted through the house, out the human being door, into the backyard, through my secret access tunnel, and around to the front. Right as Justin was about to be destroyed by the wizard, I let loose my war cry to let her know that justice was about to rain down in the form of teeth and claws.

That's when she held up a bizarre magic cylinder and shook it at me. From it came forth the most mind-numbingly terrifying sound that had ever befallen my poor ears. It was some kind of **THUNDER SCEPTER!**

I recoiled in terror, coupled with embarrassment at cowering while I was supposed to be protecting Justin. I had failed him.

Justin leaped to my side. "Wow, I'm so sorry he's acting like this."

"It's okay," said the wizard. "My mom showed me that if you put coins in an old can and shake it, you can scare off dogs who might bite you. There used to be a mean dog on this street, so I had it in my backpack."

"That's a cool trick."

"Thanks. I can tell your dog wouldn't bite me, though. I think he's just jealous. It means he really likes you."

"How'd you learn so much about dogs?"

"My mom's a vet. I want to be one too when I grow up."

She looked back at me and I scowled at her.

"Maybe it's my cat," she added. "He must smell her on me or something."

Her cat? Way to deflect! I like cats. My

second-best friend is a cat!

"I don't know what got into him," Justin said. "He's usually not aggressive."

"It's okay. I'm fine," said the evil wizard. "It's weird, because dogs usually love me."

There's that word again. Mike's word. "Dog." I have no idea what a dog even is, but I do know that if Mike used it, it must be something awful. And Justin, apologizing to her? Why, that ungrateful— I risk my life to save him, and he sides with *her*?

I wanted to bite her, I swear I did, but I feared her fiendish thunder scepter with every fiber of my being. Not only that, but I smelled her joy at stroking my fur. Why was she happy about being nice to me? Was this another spell?

Then suddenly, through scratching my belly, she **TOOK CONTROL OF MY REAR LEG** and made it stomp faster than ever before.

Justin ran off, but quickly returned with a deck of cards just like Phoebe's and they went to play on the back patio. I would have tried to stop them, but I was barely aware they were even talking, because she was still somehow puppeteering my leg via my belly, working me like a flimsy marionette. And the more she scratched, the more my foot pounded. It was appalling and simultaneously . . . *heavenly*.

It was strange, though. Even though I was sure she was an evil wizard, I could smell what I thought was *genuine affection* coming from her—not only toward Justin, but toward me as well. I shook off the doubt. This must be part of her magic.

What happened next is still a blur. All I know is that Justin and Phoebe played their card game for a couple hours, and I lay on the cool patio tiles, recovering from my defeat.

After she left—and my head had cleared—I was able to formulate a plan to save Justin:

Every wizard I've ever seen on TV has a source

of their power, a crystal ball or a wand or a staff or something. Take away the power source and the spells fail. When the spells fail, the wizard is rendered helpless. All I have to do is steal her magical power source, but what is it?

Wait. Of course! *That thunder scepter!* Next time I see her, I will take it away from her. Afterwards I will destroy the cursed thing. It will not be easy, but I have to save Justin.

That evening, as Justin and I lay in bed, he mentioned the incident with Phoebe.

"Sam, you can't go attacking Phoebe like that."

He was right, of course. I'm going to have to destroy her thunder scepter first, *then* attack her.

"I mean, she's my new friend. And if you keep acting like a jerk, she won't want to come around anymore."

Exactly, Justin. No more being a jerk. My mistake. We have to lure her back.

"Anyway, I love you buddy. Just don't mess this up, okay? Please?"

I promise I won't, dear friend. I *will* conquer this evil wizard for you. Then I clicked at him. Justin clicked back and smiled. Then came scratchies.

It feels good to be on the same page.

DAY 8

DEAR DIARY,

As I watched Justin leave for school today, I saw the wizard join him on the sidewalk. She showed him the thunder scepter. She shook it a little, and they laughed, and then she put it back in her backpack. And when she saw me in the window, she waved, all nice. The big faker.

But that's okay. I, too, was faking it.

My plan was now set in motion. After they left, I grabbed a snack from Meow's magic sand oven (okay, two snacks, but trust me, it's hard to eat just one) then made a list of foes.

With this ever-growing list of enemies, I knew

I would need help. I didn't know where to turn, but luckily the answer was right under my nose: Meow. (Like, literally. He was under my nose.)

After language class I asked him if he wanted to be my sidekick, and he said yes.

He followed me around all morning as I patrolled the house and grounds, looking for danger. I expounded on my expectations of him as he took up the mantle of sidekick.

I didn't want to overwhelm poor Meow with all his sidekick duties, so I cut it short. I figure he has enough to think about for now.

Next, Meow and I ran a patrol to the side yard, and I noticed that the muscle-bound warrior guy who'd been arguing with Lady Snakehair had been *turned to stone!*

Then it all came to me in a rush. She has snakes for hair and can turn people to *stone?* How could I have missed it?! Clearly, what we're dealing with here is a *medusa.*

Meanwhile, oblivious to the danger he was in, Meow sat at the edge of the yard. I saw the medusa lower her glasses as she slowly turned to look at Meow.

"Awww, hello there Mr. Whiskers, you wittle cutie pootie woot," she said. "Here, kitty kitty kitty."

Oh no! She was going to turn Meow to stone! Luckily, I blasted across the lawn, covered his eyes, and tackled him to the ground before he could meet her gaze. I would not allow him to become a stone trophy in this evil garden of doom.

Poor Meow reacted in confusion and fear, but at least he's alive. I will explain it all to him tomorrow morning, after language class.

I knew I couldn't meet her evil glare, so I closed my eyes. But I also knew I had to tackle this gorgon before she petrified me—or worse, Justin!

When I woke up, I was lying on the peeing couch with Gary and Elaine standing over me. I'm not sure exactly what happened, but I'm pretty sure I took out the medusa. In the process I must have accidentally glanced at her. Being almost petrified by a medusa, by the way, feels kind of like hitting a cement wall with your head. Frankly, I was lucky to be alive at all.

"What do you think?" Gary asked Elaine as they stared down at me, concerned.

"I think he's a goofball."

"Yeah, but other than that," Gary pressed.

"He seems okay. Pupils are fine," she said, shining a light in my eyes. "Just a bump on the head."

My head was killing me, but I'm not one to rest on my laurels, so I was up and around the house again within minutes.

I ran outside to check for Lady Snakehair's body, but there wasn't any sign of her. Hopefully she disintegrated upon impact with my head.

I spent the rest of the day ruminating on how good it was not to be a petrified garden ornament, while taking full advantage of the chewing chair.

DAY 9

DEAR DIARY,

First thing this morning, my feline sidekick and I watched as Justin gathered up all of the family's most precious treasures in a white bag.

It was clear from the delicious scent emanating from the bag that it was everything the Petersons hold dear. So you can imagine my confusion when Justin put the glorious bag in a treasure chest (which is where it belongs) but then wheeled it outside to the curb (where it most certainly does *not* belong).

I tried to tell him that the side of the road was a terrible place to put the treasure chest, but he

would have none of it. Justin ushered us inside. But Meow and I had other plans. We had to protect the treasures before anyone could come along and take them.

For an hour we sat there, keeping vigil. Making Meow my sidekick was already paying off, for he saw the great enemy ship approaching before I did, and warned me of the impending danger. **PIRATES.**

I had never seen *land* pirates or a ship like this one before, but as sure as my name is **NO SAM!** I knew that's what they were.

Two clues validated my hypothesis:

1. They were stopping at every house on the street and stealing everyone's treasure out of their treasure chests. Classic pirate behavior. They even had a giant arm that would lift the treasure chests and just empty them into their ship.

2. The captain had a patch over one eye.

I'll be cursed if I let pirates steal the Petersons' treasure, even if I have to eat it all myself. So that's just what I decided to do. Fast-thinking Meow realized my plan and jumped in to help. But the pirates caught on and came down upon us.

They brandished brooms and shovels like spears and axes—obviously low-level pirates, unable to afford proper weaponry. And while I respect their need for treasure so they can upgrade their weapons, I was nonetheless steadfast in my duty to protect the Petersons' booty.

I held my ground, but Meow maneuvered himself into a hasty retreat.

89

Just as the brigands were about to move in for
the kill, an incredible thing happened.

As soon as Justin pulled me to safety, the
pirates picked up the remaining treasure and
stole every last piece of it.

"Sorry guys! Won't happen again," Gary apologized to the pirates.

Wait. **WHAT?? DID HE JUST
APOLOGIZE TO THE PIRATES?!**

Why don't you just invite them into your house

and offer them a cup of coffee while you're at it?

"Hey guys," Gary added. "How about I make it up to you? I just made a fresh pot of coffee if you want some."

OH MY GOSH!

"Sorry, Dr. Peterson," said one of the pirates, with what was clearly false politeness. "We've got a schedule to keep. But no worries. Have a good day!"

Have a good day? They've got a schedule to keep? Oh, these pirates are good, but not good enough to fool me. And Gary is a doctor? I sure wouldn't want him as *my* physician.

As they led me inside, though, I heard Gary talk about how the pirates would be back and how Justin would have to contain me. I appreciate his concern for my safety, but as long as there are thieving pirates on our street, I have to protect the Peterson family booty.

After everything calmed down, I held an emergency meeting with Meow and together we

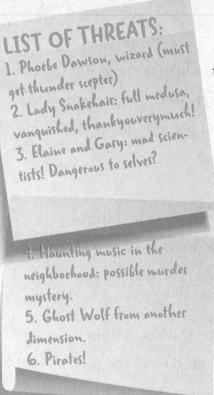

LIST OF THREATS:
1. Phoebe Dawson, wizard (must get thunder scepter)
2. Lady Snakehair: full medusa, vanquished, thankyouverymuch!
3. Elaine and Gary: mad scientists! Dangerous to selves?

4. Haunting music in the neighborhood: possible murder mystery.
5. Ghost Wolf from another dimension.
6. Pirates!

updated our threat list.

Before Meow and I could strategize, the terrible sound of *the intruder-alert alarm* sounded! All hands on deck! **BATTLE STATIONS! BATTLE STATIONS!**

"No, Sam! Hush!" said Justin. "It's just the doorbell. It's Phoebe!"

Oh, really? Just an evil, sorcery-slinging wizard here but **NO WORRIES, JUSTIN!** It's **JUST** that. At least this time I was prepared. I had set the trap this morning. Now all I had to do was spring it.

"Hi, Justin. Hiya, Sammy!"

"Hi, Phoebe!" said Justin.

Hello, *you monster.* (I didn't say it. I thought it, though.)

Are we buddies now, Sammy? Are we?

As she came in and petted me, I feared that she would use her devilish puppetry trick on me and take control of my leg. (Simultaneously, I *hoped* she would because it felt *soooo* good.)

I leapt up, grabbed the thunder scepter in my mouth, and ran!

"What the—?!" she cried.

"YEAH, 'what-the'!" I yelled back at her. "I'll what-the *you* after I wreck this scepter!"

No, Sam! Drop it! Get back here!

Never! I thought to myself! **HA HA HA HA! HAAAAAA!**

"Hey! No! Sam!" she cried.

That's right. Now you know my name.

Before Justin and Phoebe could get to me, the can was empty. I had vanquished the scepter, and it was now thunder-less. Justin was free! Take *that,* wizard! You. Are. **VANQUISHED!**

But then she smiled at me. Wait. What? She shouldn't be smiling. She was clearly a step ahead of me. And what she did next was worse than controlling my leg. More humiliating than that thunder scepter.

Oh no! A magic wand!

When she used it on me, I felt utterly compelled to catch the red light-creature that she controlled with it! Oh sweet, wonderful, tantalizing little red light! Oh irresistible and provocative little point of luminescence! But every time I had it cornered or trapped underpaw, it would magically escape my grasp. And when I touched the creature, my paws went right through it!

Even poor Meow was roused from one of his many daytime naps and began mindlessly chasing

it with me. It was truly nightmarish, as the wizard now had control of both of us. Justin, meanwhile, had been reduced to a giggling ignoramus.

"They're so cute! I do this to my cat all the time! She loves it," said the heartless monster.

But while she's clearly won *this* battle, the war is far from over. Because now, she's finally revealed the true source of her magic power. It's her magic wand.

And I know exactly how to get it.

DAY 10

DEAR DIARY,

I'm quite proud of myself. And I'll tell you why. Justin and I finished our breakfast this morning and we were outside for our daily mystery game of "Go, Sam!" when the evil wizard came walking down the sidewalk.

Oh, how I wanted to charge, but I knew she had that accursed wand on her. I slowly approached her, wagging my tail so she knew I meant no harm. Heh. Justin stood astonished as I let her pet me.

"Awww, look!" she said. "He's saying sorry for breaking the shaky can! Aww! Hi Sammy-wammy.

You're such a good boy! Who wants scratchies?"

Fine, okay, **SCRATCHIES YES!**

"He's so cute. I could eat him up," she said.

Wait. What? Did she just say she could eat me up? Suddenly, ice-cold awfulness raced through my veins. So that's her plan!

But despite this sickening realization, I maintained my composure. As I let her pet me—nay, even let her scratchies me—I nuzzled my face into her and she melted before my charms, if I do say so myself. Justin smelled of joy and satisfaction. While it made me happy to smell him so upbeat, I felt a little bit guilty, because this was all a ruse. But one I was pulling for his own good.

After they brought me back inside and left to go play cards, I spit out what I had pickpocketed from her when I'd snuggled against her.

Achievement unlocked. I had just successfully pickpocketed an evil wizard. The next time she tried to use her magic on me, she would fail in an epic fashion.

After they left, I gnawed that magic wand into a *million tiny pieces* and buried it in the backyard.

Today was mercifully quiet. I appreciated the break in the constant stream of villains and monsters that seem to flow toward the Peterson house like some kind of vortex of evil. But sadly, the calm was broken during my nightly rounds.

As I made my last evening patrol, I stepped into the back room with the sliding glass door. And there he was: Ghost Wolf.

And just like our first confrontation, it was like this hellhound could read my mind, mimic my every move. He was mocking me, drawing me closer to the mortal combat that would end one of us . . . *forever*.

As I was staring him down, who did I see climbing into our yard from the back wall? None other than Drago and Grisha! And they were clearly bringing me gifts. Probably hoagies.

But there, in that moment of generosity, they

had stumbled into the middle of my confrontation with Ghost Wolf! If they took another step, they would no doubt be consumed in his fiery maw of death! Luckily, he was focusing his attention on something behind me.

And thankfully, they saw me.

These are good men, with kind hearts. They like food and laughter and friendship. By no means could they have faced something as dangerous as a Ghost Wolf. I had to get them to flee, so I unleashed a volley of loud warnings.

At the same time, Ghost Wolf began barking at something behind me, but I dared not look back to see what it was, or he would surely strike me down. Luckily, Drago and Grisha fled for their lives. I continued barking even after they'd left, and so did Ghost Wolf, until we were interrupted by Justin, Gary, and Elaine.

It was like living some kind of terribly frustrating déjà vu. The Petersons could not see ghosts, but that was all right. The most important thing is that I saved the lives of Drago and Grisha.

My friends.

DAY 11

DEAR DIARY,

This morning, before anyone got up, I went to the back door to look for the Ghost Wolf. No sign. From this, I can hypothesize two things:

1. Maybe the monster can only come out at night, like vampires and Santa Claus.
2. Possibly, and quite likely, I have driven him off forever.

Regardless, I will be checking the door for him periodically, just to be safe.

After a quiet breakfast, Justin ran off with Phoebe again. Knowing I had destroyed her wand, I was confident in letting him go.

On my morning rounds, I noticed something that completely wrecked me. Next door, Lady Snakehair was working in her garden! How had she survived my death charge? Then I saw what she had placed in her garden.

First of all, I didn't even know that frogs wore waistcoats. Or glasses. Or that they could grow to such enormous sizes.

I would have mounted a rescue operation immediately, but while the creature looked gentle, one never knows. The last thing I wanted was to free a frog twice my size, only to discover that he was a worse character than the medusa from which I had rescued him. Besides, my main duty was to the Petersons.

Hmmm. Clearly, running with my eyes closed like last time wasn't going to work. Ah ha! I had it.

Blast it! A freeze cannon, of course! Fool me once, shame on you, fool me twice and . . . well, there won't be a twice, *Lady Snakehair!* That freeze cannon is going down, eventually. First, I had to dry off and warm up. Freeze cannons are super . . . freeze-y.

This evening, as I was curled up in bed next to Justin, Elaine and Gary came into the room and stood looking at us.

Wait a minute. What? Sure, Justin was all of these things and more, but were they seriously thinking of getting rid of him?

Gary: "I know. But look how good he is for him. He really makes him happy."

It's true. Justin does make me happy.

Elaine: "I just don't see how we could get rid of him without breaking the poor kid's heart."

Wow. They're keeping Justin just for me.

Gary: "I guess. But something has to be done about his behavior."

Elaine: "Yeah, but who has time to train him when we're so close to finishing this?"

Gary: "Not us. Justin."

Elaine: "Hmm. It would be good for him to have some responsibility."

Gary: "And if he can't improve the dog's behavior, I'm sorry to say we'll just have to take him back to the shelter."

Jeez. Calling Justin a dog? And threatening to take him to a shelter? That's low, even for Gary.

Elaine: "Let's talk to him tomorrow."

And with that, they left the room as quietly as they'd entered. I only hope that Justin will learn to behave, for his own sake. Although, to be honest, I've never seen him do anything wrong, so the whole encounter has left me completely confused. But then again, I am always confused when dealing with Gary and Elaine.

Maybe I can get him to start using the pooping rug or the peeing couch.

DAY 12

DEAR DIARY,

Today started unusually, because Gary and Elaine were actually at breakfast in the eating room.

"Justin, we're making incredible progress in the lab," said Elaine.

"Yeah," said Gary, "we should be ready for our first trial in the next week."

"Justin," his mom said, "we just wanted to say thanks for being so patient with us. We're sorry we haven't been around lately."

"Sam's been keeping you company though, right?" said Gary.

Justin just looked down at me and I clicked

at him. He clicked back and smiled. He snuck me some bacon and I was in heaven.

"I also made a new friend, and she's really cool," Justin said.

Suddenly, I was pulled from my bacon reverie by the sound of the door slamming. When I looked up, Justin was gone. Wait. What? I ran to the viewing platform at the front window to look out at the street.

And as always, there she was: the wizard, standing at the end of our walkway, smiling and being all evil-wizard-y.

Wait a minute! I'd destroyed the wand! How was he still under her control? I could see the hunger in her eyes. And I could smell a nervous anticipation coming from her too.

Oh no! Hungry? Nervous? This was it! Today she was going to eat Justin!

I started pawing at the handle of the front door. I didn't have grabby things on my hands like naked-monkey-things do, but I had to try.

Holy moly! She wasn't going to eat him. She was going to poison him. I knew I had to act, and fast! I used my patented two-handed digging method, and miracle of miracles, I opened the door and broke the spell! Justin ran to me and scooped me up.

"Whoa, there! What's going on buddy?" Justin

said in my ear. "I thought you and Phoebe were pals now."

Not while she's doing this to you, the one person in my life I've ever really cared about.

As he took me back to the house, the wizard spoke, as if to taunt me.

"Hey Justin, have you seen my laser pointer?"

"No. You lose it?"

"Yeah. Weird. I wonder where it is?"

It's in a thousand pieces and buried in a very deep grave, where it belongs.

Justin put me back in the house and closed the door. The wizard smiled and waved at me from the street. It was her way of letting me know I'd missed the target again. Clearly the wand is not the source of her power, but if not the wand, then what?

And that's when I noticed it. As Justin walked away, he was eating the candy bar that Phoebe had given him. And he wasn't dead. Or sick. Or transforming into a mutant. He was just happy and normal and okay. And she was eating it too, and she was also fine. And they both smelled like joy.

Could I have been . . . *wrong* about her? Clearly the candy was okay to eat. It confounded and vexed me.

Look how confounded and vexed I was!

confounded + vexed

I had to shake the doubt away again. *Of course* she's an evil wizard. The evidence against her is too strong. Also, watching them eat a candy bar gave me the munchies, and I knew exactly where to find some.

After indulging in a few cookies from Meow's magic sand oven, I discovered that Gary and Elaine have been using the front hall closet as some kind of holding cell for their latest scientific monstrosity.

Is this the breakthrough that they were talking about at breakfast? But why would they build a deadly assassination robot? Because

assassination ROBOT

they're mad scientists, that's why. But mad or not, they are my wards to protect.

Sadly, the story got worse, because next I saw Elaine take the monstrosity out, power it up, and dance with it. Yes. Dance. Around the *entire* house.

Finally, after what seemed like hours of screaming and yelling, I convinced Elaine to power it down. After which she put it back in its cell. As I began to consider how I would destroy this monster, the front door opened! It was Justin!

"Hey there, buddy!!" Justin said, "You miss me?!"

Of course I missed him. I always miss him.

"I missed you too! Oh! And look what I got ya, Sam! I figured if you had a nice chew toy, you'd maybe stop misbehaving so much. And also maybe take out your aggression on this thing instead of Phoebe."

I might've guessed this had something to do with *her*. First of all, this dead animal was clearly a victim of one of Phoebe's dark spells. And now she was sending it to me via Justin as some kind

of sick warning—a warning that *I was next*.

It looked like it might've once been a squirrel, but it was so flat now that it was almost unidentifiable. Also, the dead thing was smiling, which added to my confusion.

And then Justin swung it in my face. He swung the DEAD CORPSE OF A MURDERED SQUIRREL . . . IN MY FACE.

"Get it! Get it!" he yelled.

Frankly, I was offended.

I don't like to go to bed mad, but sometimes there's no other option. I mean, everyone has their limits, right? And now I know mine.

It's when someone swings
a dead squirrel in my face.

119

DAY 13

DEAR DIARY,

When I woke up, I was still angry at Justin for swinging that dead body in my face. There was no school, so thankfully there was no wizard this morning. And I could tell Justin felt bad about being the messenger for Phoebe's deadly warning.

I never wanted anything to come between Justin and me, so when we were in the backyard I brought him a stick as a peace offering. I know he's been under a lot of stress lately, and if he's anything like me, he'll enjoy chewing on a stick for a few hours. But to my utter confusion, as soon as I gave it to him, he threw the thing as far as he could.

"Go get it, Sam!"

Go get it? What the heck? I just *had* it.

At first, I was offended. I'd picked that nice chewing stick out for him myself. He must have thrown it by accident. At any rate, I raced out as fast as I could and brought it back to him. He smiled, took it from me, and patted me on the head.

"Good job!" he said.

Then he threw it again. Again, I was confused. But again, I brought it back. Something was obviously wrong with his arm, and he couldn't control it.

After retrieving the stick fifteen or twenty times, I was getting exhausted, so I kept it. But then he started chasing me and laughing. So I ran. I have to admit, it was fun, but he was *not* getting that stick back. Eventually he just laughed and clicked at me. I clicked back, and he went inside. I decided that, to avoid this embarrassing situation again, I would eat the stick.

I was feeling better about the Justin situation.

But it seems like every time I put out one fire around here, another one starts up. This next particular blaze, though, came not from a threat to the Petersons, but from my own dark past.

It happened later in the morning while I was on a routine patrol of the neighborhood. I rounded a corner, and there he was.

Mike.

There are many things in this world that I am not scared of. I can handle medusas, pirates, assassination robots, evil wizards, and even ghost wolves from beyond the spirit realm. But Mike— Mike *really* frightens me.

Maybe it's because when I face the other threats, I am doing it to defend the people I love. But Mike is a threat to my very existence. I guess it's just easier to be brave when you're protecting someone else.

Needless to say, when I saw Mike, I ran.

When I got home, and my heart finally stopped racing, I decided that I would restrict future patrols to just the Peterson house and yard. I could not risk running into Mike again.

I guess if there's a silver lining to this episode, it comes in the form of a cat. When I was at my lowest point, who was it that came to cheer me up? Good ol' Meow.

Sweet, thoughtful Meow. With his simple, homespun wisdom, he made me realize that I couldn't hide from my troubles, and that life had to go on. I decided to crawl out of my despair and give Meow his language class for the day.

While I was busy with Meow, I overheard Justin talking on the phone. He obviously recognizes my human-to-cat bond with Meow, because I heard him telling Phoebe on the other end of the line that I loved our pet cat. (Although he called Meow "Mr. Whiskers," which was odd. You'd think the boy would at least know the name of our pet cat.)

Then, for some inexplicable reason, Phoebe brought her cat over to play with me.

First off, calling that walking pestilence to humanity a cat is stretching the truth to its breaking point. Phoebe said the thing's name was "Mrs. Muffity Puff," but I think Razor-Claw-Death-Beast would be a far more fitting name.

All I did was say hello and inspect her, like I do all new people I meet.

To say that Mrs. Muffity Puff's response was an overreaction is an understatement.

She chose to pull what I think was a knife on me, even though I never saw her draw it, nor did I actually see the blade. Maybe the cat had an invisible knife.

Either way, she cut my nose and I reacted instinctively, albeit poorly.

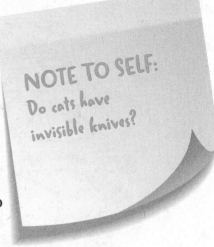

NOTE TO SELF:
Do cats have
invisible knives?

The playdate might have been salvaged if our curtains were strong enough to hold a cat.

Which they weren't. Or if cats loved being submerged in warm water.

Which they don't.

After everything calmed down, Justin apologized to Phoebe, and Phoebe calmed down her Razor-Claw-Death-Beast and they left.

I thought about how the cat had instantly hated me.

And then it occurred to me. Phoebe's cat *isn't* a cat at all! It's Phoebe's *familiar,* the source of her power! All evil wizards have a familiar. And this must be hers! Phoebe's real intention had been for that thing to kill me with one swipe of its invisible knife!

I have finally discovered the *true* source of Phoebe's evil magic power. And because of her misstep, I can now make a plan to be rid of that familiar—and thus, the wizard it powers—forever.

Tonight, while being especially careful to keep an eye out for Mike, I decided to go outside and take in some fresh air while I made my plans for Mrs. Muffity Puff (if that even *is* her real name). Unfortunately, I saw something that was too distracting to ignore.

What kind of fiend would petrify a naked baby . . . while he was peeing? If I didn't stop this snake-haired monster soon, Justin would surely end up in that garden of frozen death.

To get to the medusa, I had to avoid two things:

1. Her petrifying gaze attack
2. Her exceedingly shocking freeze cannon

Well, there's not a lot that can be done about the gaze. When I next confront her, I will just have to do my best not to look her in the eye. But as for the freeze cannon . . .

It occurred to me that if I could somehow turn the medusa's gaze against her, *I* could petrify *her*. Ah ha! I will execute my plan tomorrow . . .

131

DAY 14

DEAR DIARY,

My enemy's enemy is my friend.

Justin, *again,* put the delicious family treasure out in the front yard despite my protests. I
swear, it's as if the pirates come every week. It
seems that Justin, as well as all the neighbors, is
putting out the treasure chests for them on purpose. If it keeps up, at this rate, the Petersons will
be facing complete financial ruin.

Before running off with Phoebe to play cards,
Justin put me in the backyard, but he hadn't
anticipated my hidden security access tunnel.

I decided to sit and wait in plain sight. Maybe,

if I could make myself look extra ferocious, I could thwart the pirates with my mere presence.

The pirates rounded the corner. They were beginning to steal the treasures from every house on the street. Again. And then Meow came out, carrying something in his mouth.

Good heavens, it was Justin's dead squirrel. And to my dismay, Meow dropped the awful thing at my feet and looked at me. I asked him if it was his intent to give the squirrel a proper burial. He said yes. At that point, Meow put his paw on the dead body, presumably to say a prayer before we buried it, and in the following surreal, world-shattering moment, everything in our universe exploded. Because when he touched the dead thing, *it screamed at us!*

IT WAS A ZOMBIE!

We fled and hid in the backyard. But then I remembered the pirates! They were stealing the family treasure, and I could do nothing to stop them, blocked off by the undead! One of the pirates dumped our treasure in the hull of their land ship. Then the most bizarre thing happened.

I could have warned them that it wasn't a rat. But I just let them touch the zombie. I hoped it would strike, but it did not. It must've been biding its time.

As the pirates sailed away, I had to smile, just a little. Those thieving buccaneers would soon be bitten and die horrible zombie-squirrel deaths. So thank you, Mr. Undead Squirrel. My enemy's enemy is my friend.

Next, it was time to deal with my friend's enemy—who also, incidentally, is my enemy, in addition to being the enemy of my friend. Or something.

Everything was going according to plan. I had the mirror, the freeze cannon was disabled, and all I had to do was get the villain to look in the mirror and the potential Peterson petrification problem would be solved forever.

Lady Snakehair heard my charge and ran for the freeze cannon, but *ah ha!* It was useless.

Just when she thought she had me, I leapt up and escaped her deadly glare!

Oh no! The very weapon with which I would destroy the medusa had now destroyed the poor naked peeing baby! Pee went flying everywhere.

Not one of my proudest moments.

I knew instantly that I had to save that innocent child. I dropped the mirror, but was able to break naked-peeing-baby's fall.

The villain survived, but the day was saved, for naked-peeing-baby had been spared from shattering on the stony ground below. I made a hasty retreat. There was no point in battling the medusa without my mirror.

"Another day!" I shouted over my shoulder as I escaped via my security access tunnel.

DAY 15

DEAR DIARY,

I discovered a new and terrible thing today. An ominous threat to the family that chills me to the bone.

Mere days after I neutralized Elaine's heat cannon, the neighborhood gets besieged by . . . a *Popsicle monster!*

Everyone was already eating what looked to be pieces of this frozen abomination. Was that his trick? Victims would eat from his flesh, only to fall into a dazed state . . . and then what? Be attacked by the icy beast?

I knew that underneath that lie of a smile was the heart of a wintery predator, hell-bent on eating us all. But not today! I was about to charge when I realized something. There was Phoebe, with her familiar. *Two birds with one stone.*

As I looked at the landscape before me, like a great general, I saw the field of battle. I saw two great enemies. I saw angles and tactics. I saw the road to victory, the risks that needed to be taken, the potential failure and sacrifice. And then . . . I acted.

I knew I was running into battle against two of the most dangerous foes I had ever faced.

This battle would decide who lived and died. And for Justin, I would do either. Because I love him.

I would allow my enemy to think it was escaping . . .

. . . when in fact, I was only driving it into lethal confrontation with another enemy. Two birds with one stone.

Guaranteeing their mutual destruction.

It was hard to watch the Popsicle monster eat the wizard's familiar right in front of her. It was also difficult to witness the icy beast as it spasmed and lurched in a final dance of death. A deadly last meal, indeed, for *you,* Popsicle monster!

Dark choices were made, but for the greater good.

I saw the Popsicle monster's corpse, lifeless on the battlefield. On this day, I—NO SAM!—was a hero. For I had defeated two of my greatest foes.

But then suddenly I was overcome with the smell of anguish. I don't know if you've ever smelled anguish, but it's like happiness dying. Like a friendship ending. And it wasn't just coming from Justin.

It was also coming from Phoebe. And that totally confused me. If she was really an evil wizard, why would she be heartbroken?

Even though I had won today, I felt terrible, because I had accidentally gotten . . . *three* birds with one stone.

Phoebe, please let me help!

Just go be with your dog! I don't want to see you again!

I was in the yard as the sun set, the stars taking their places overhead, when I smelled great anxiety coming from Drago and Grisha's van parked on the street. My friends. If ever I needed them, it was now. But they smelled worried. Additionally, I smelled steak.

I think my tail wagging and smiles finally calmed them. And they were so relaxed afterward that they even gave me my own *whole raw steak!*

As soon as I was done eating, I used the security access tunnel and made it into the house through the human door. But I suddenly felt so drowsy . . . Wow. Steaks are exhausting!

After one of the heaviest sleeps of my life, I woke up in the middle of the night to a real ripper of a headache. Justin had covered me with a little blanket and let me sleep where I was.

When I got up and walked around, all was still and silent, as it should be, but something didn't smell right. Like, literally. It smelled like Drago and Grisha in here. It also smelled like that slightly burn-y, oily, plastic and electronics scent from their van.

I ran to the window. Their van was gone. Something was terribly wrong. Drago and Grisha came into the Petersons' house tonight, and I'd slept through it!

First, I ran to see that Justin was okay.

Thank goodness he was safe. I couldn't help but melt a little when I saw him sleep.

Then I checked on Gary and Elaine. Everyone was okay. Of course. Drago and Grisha were our friends. But why had they been in the house?

Next, I ran around the entire residence, sniffing out all the spots that smelled like Drago and Grisha and their van, and I found tiny machines all over the place.

Using my superior reasoning, I concluded that these little objects could only be one thing: game pieces! Obviously, Drago and Grisha wanted to play a game. A scavenger hunt game!

But something was weird. Gary and Elaine were upstairs in bed, but they apparently left the door to the lab ajar. And they never do that. *Hmm.* And did Drago and Grisha have lab access clearance? They must, because I could smell them all over the place.

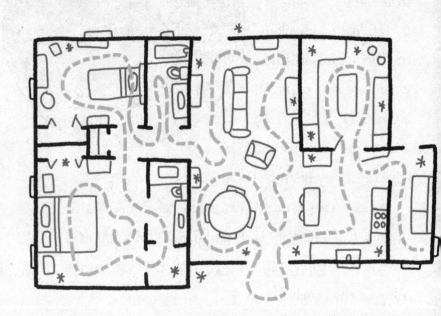

I decided to continue the scavenger hunt in the lab. And it's a good thing, too, because there were little game pieces on each of the phones, Elaine's computer, Gary's computer, the front and back doors—all over the lab! The Petersons would never be able to see these little things, but I could smell them, no problem.

It took all night, but I sniffed out all of the little game pieces and ate them up. They're going to be so happy when they find out I played their game!

DAY 16

DEAR DIARY,

I woke up this morning with the worst stomach pain. At first I thought it was guilt because I had hurt Justin when I got rid of Phoebe. But I knew he would get over it when her spells slowly wore off, and he'd thank me for saving his life.

Then I thought it was all those game pieces I ate, because I kept burping up that burn-y, plastic-y taste. I might have stayed in all day nursing it, but Meow reminded me that we had patrols to do.

Before I could even make it past the chewing chair, I collapsed in agony. Meow saw my troubles

and immediately ran for help. Trusty Meow.

But the pain suddenly grew so bad that I think I passed out, for after that, all I remember was falling on the soft carpet and everything going black.

MOM! DAD!
Come quick!

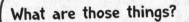

156

I woke up in some kind of prison in yet another mad scientist's lab. When I looked around, I saw other victims of the scientist's evil surgeries.

It seemed as though we had all been modified into cyborgs. I could tell by the strange neck pieces with which we had all been fitted. Half-human and half-machine, all of us.

It didn't take long for me to realize what the cybernetic cone was for. While clumsy and somewhat cumbersome, it did amplify my hearing. I could hear the mad scientist and his minions having discussions on the other side of their lair.

But if the surgery was to connect my cybernetic hearing cone, why did my *stomach* have stitches in it? I couldn't see them because of the cone, but I could feel them, and they itched terribly.

That night, after all the other prisoners were asleep, I heard another conversation. It wasn't the evil scientist, though. It was Drago and Grisha!

Drago and Grisha, here to rescue me! I started calling out to let them know where I was. The other caged humans also called out for help.

Unfortunately, they couldn't hear us, because they never came to rescue me. I did hear them leave, though.

The operation failed for some reason, so I would just have to wait.

DAY 17

DEAR DIARY,

Sure enough, today Justin and Gary came to get me. Justin held me so hard it almost hurt, but that's okay. I loved it anyway. I didn't ever want to be away from him again. Even for a day.

After a routine house patrol, I came back inside to find Justin staring out the front window. He missed Phoebe, I could smell it. I decided to get him a big, long stick from the yard to cheer him up.

"No, Sam. But thanks, buddy. I'm just not in the mood."

His sadness was killing me. I tried clicking.

No return click. He just stared gloomily out the window.

Then the doubt started to creep in. Doubt about Phoebe. I started to think about all those times when I was confused about her maybe *not* being an evil wizard. What if that confusion *wasn't* her baffling magic, but my own brain telling me not to be ridiculous? I decided to check my notes.

1. The candy bar she gave Justin: not poisoned, just a yummy treat she wanted to share with him.

2. And what about when she gave me scratchies? I could smell she was happy doing it.

3. And then there was her heartbreak when she got mad at Justin. Evil wizards just don't get heartbroken (no hearts, you'll remember).

I mean, there are three strikes against the evil wizard theory, and it was right under my nose the whole time. What if, heaven forbid, I'd maybe, *possibly,* been wrong about Phoebe?! What if the *seemingly* sweet girl was really just an *actually* sweet girl?

Oh no. If that were true, then it would be the single greatest mistake of my career. I shuddered at the thought. That would mean I'd also caused the destruction of a regular (albeit really mean and ugly) cat.

I decided to go outside and try and get my thoughts in order.

All was quiet around the yard's perimeter. I sniffed around for Drago and Grisha. I could really use some friendly advice about all of this. I couldn't smell them, but the cone allowed me to hear them talking from inside their van down the street, so I immediately headed there.

Outside the back door, I saw one of the little game pieces they'd left all over the Peterson's house. Strangely, it smelled like me. I decided to return it to them.

I smelled them inside. Was this a game of hide-and-seek now? Jeez. These two never stop having fun. Well, I wasn't in the mood for games, so I left their piece on the stoop.

On the way home, I made an amazing discovery about my cyborg hearing cone. When I got to the backyard, I saw a strange creature sitting on a stump by the bushes.

What I discovered is that not only does this implant enhance my hearing, it also amplifies my voice. You see, when I yell, the sound is more powerful than any weapon I have ever witnessed.

All I meant to do was yell at the strange little fella, but I completely disintegrated him! I have *sonic bark power!*

This fully explains the stitches in my stomach. They've implanted a sonic barker in me, combining it with the cone to make my bark a deadly superweapon! Tonight, my enemies—the enemies to the Petersons—would all tremble before me.

When night came, there was a crackle in the air—a sensation that something big was about to happen. With a newfound confidence, the kind that only comes with having sonic bark disintegration powers, I marched next door to the medusa's lair to finish her, once and for all. I could already savor the sweet nectar of victory as I prepared to bark her house down—and then, exposing her,

I'd bark her straight back to whatever evil dimension she'd crawled out of.

But the taste of winning quickly slipped away, replaced by the terror of seeing my worst nightmare made real . . .

She got *MEOW!* Poor Meow! Sensitive, caring, tender, intelligent Meow! Meow, who only spoke one word, but whose heart had a vocabulary of love like no other.

I wanted to disintegrate her right then and there! But it occurred to me that my bark could be so powerful, it would turn all of these poor statues to dust. And I could not risk that, least of all sweet, loyal Meow.

I would rescue him first. But I found that even though I was able to drag Meow with my jaws, it was hard to get him up the little hill between the Petersons' yard and Lady Snakehair's yard. More than hard, actually. It was impossible.

MEOW!

Oh no! Maybe, I thought, I could fix Meow. He was only broken in two pieces, after all. It couldn't possibly get worse, I thought. But then . . .

The rest is a blur.

In the midst of my darkest moment, I smelled something familiar. It was Mrs. Muffity Puff. She was alive and out there in the neighborhood somewhere! But how could that be? I saw her eaten by the giant Popsicle only two days ago. What if she'd somehow survived? More importantly—what if she'd survived and was only a regular cat?

If my earlier suspicion was correct, and Phoebe was just a girl and not an evil wizard, that would mean Mrs. Muffity Puff was just a plain old cat and not her familiar.

And if Phoebe was a girl, and her cat was a cat, then Justin could safely be alone with Phoebe without any danger of being eaten. And that would make him happy.

There 'it was! I knew what I had to do. I—NO SAM!—had to find that scent trail again and rescue Mrs. Muffity Puff.

But as I turned to begin my quest, who was there but . . . Mike!

There you are! I've been looking everywhere for you!

I thought, this can not be happening. Mike threw me in his car and took me back to his place. Oh, misery! Oh, horrible fate! I am truly fortune's fool!

After all I had been through, I was going to end up alone in Mike's apartment. Worse, I would never see Justin again.

After Mike was gone, I tried to open the door— but again, no hands. I even tried the window.

Heck, I even tried to dig under the door, but all I managed was to scratch up the floor. Mike would not be happy about that.

I tried everything I could think of, even using my sonic cyber cone to bark down the door, but Mike was one step ahead of me. He had installed sonic-bark-proof doors and windows.

As I sat there, I heard a scratching at the door. Mike was home? He usually stayed out a lot longer when he went out. I decided when the door opened, I would bolt past him and flee again. As it opened, I launched myself from the couch. But it wasn't Mike at all . . .

Glory oh glory, it was my two pals! They'd come to rescue me, because of course they did!

I didn't hear a word they said because I was so elated to see them.

Strangely, though, they weren't taking me home. They had planned some sort of surprise road trip party for me. But I couldn't celebrate with them quite yet; I had too much left to do.

Somehow, even though I thought I was being perfectly clear in telling them to turn the van around and take me home, they just tossed me a steak!

I ate it, of course, because, c'mon, *steak*. But before I could get back to my protests, I suddenly grew so tired. Something about steak . . . that just makes me . . . so . . . sleepy . . . huh . . .

DAY 18

DEAR DIARY,

Meow was gone. Mrs. Muffity Puff was missing. But most of all, Justin's heart was broken. And it was all my fault.

Even though I had been saved from Mike, I was now stuck in a cage on some kind of joy ride with Drago and Grisha. While I appreciated the rescue, the timing could not have been worse.

I sat up and looked around. It was morning. Drago was still driving, and Grisha was in the front seat, sleeping. Outside I saw a gray wasteland of abandoned factories. How could I get them to take me seriously?

That's when I noticed that Drago seemed to be making the van go with his foot on a small thing on the floor. If I could just somehow bark at what I will call the "gas pedal," for lack of a better term, then I could disintegrate it and the van would roll to a peaceful stop. The trick would be focusing my bark ray on the pedal without also disintegrating Drago's foot.

I focused and barked as loud as I could, being careful to aim at the "gas pedal" and not Drago's foot.

Bullseye! I didn't actually see the "gas pedal" disintegrate, but clearly, Drago must have panicked that it was suddenly gone and tried to pull the van over to the side of the road.

After that, everything was a spinning, sliding confusion as my cage spun around. Then the van doors were thrown open and out went the cage, which tumbled about in the grass. When I stood up and got my bearings, I saw that the cage doors had broken open.

I'm happy to say Drago's foot was still at the end of his leg and not disintegrated. My aim had been perfect. Thank goodness he and Grisha were okay, if a little banged up. They'd be disappointed that we had to end our joy ride, but I would explain later.

Now I just had to find my way home.

I spent the whole day and most of the night running in bigger and bigger circles all around town, hoping to catch home's familiar scent. I was shocked not to have gotten a whiff of the Petersons, especially considering what a stinky bunch they are.

(As a side note, twice I had to go to the bathroom in the grass, for lack of a pooping rug. I'm embarrassed to admit I'm taking a liking to it.)

Just as the sun was about to rise, I caught the sound of yipping and growling in the distance. I would have ignored it entirely, except for one thing. Coming from the same direction was the scent of Mrs. Muffity Puff!

I came to a fence with a hole in it. On the other side was Mrs. Muffity Puff. She was on the roof of a car that was surrounded by the most horrible-looking predators I had ever laid eyes on.

I'd never seen creatures quite like these before. I'm fairly certain they were lions. I had to save that cat and get her home. It was time to disintegrate some lions.

Even as they trotted toward me, I prepared to annihilate them all. But then the worst thing happened. My cyber cone got stuck!

The lions were closing in on me! I didn't have time to aim my sonic bark ray properly. Trying my best not to destroy Mrs. Muffity Puff in the background, I let loose the loudest bark I could.

Good heavens! I'd missed the lions and destroyed an entire building!

When the dust cleared, I realized the building had been totally decimated. Luckily, even though I'd missed them, the lions had scattered. Clearly, I had overwhelmed them with my powers.

Mrs. Muffity Puff was so shaken that she cow-ered beneath me. I had finally won her over.

When I asked her if she was okay, all she could do was shower me with affection and say "Meow" over and over again.

Meow! Poor Meow. And the Petersons! They were at home, completely vulnerable without me there to protect them!

I set off, with Mrs. Muffity Puff close behind. We wandered for hours. By afternoon, I'm happy to report, I'd picked up on the sweet smell of home—or, more specifically, the stinky smell of Justin's socks.

If we walked all night, we could be there by morning.

DAY 19

DEAR DIARY,

After walking through the night, Mrs. Muffity Puff and I were exhausted and starved—even after regretfully robbing someone of the contents of their treasure chest. (That said, we only took what we needed to survive, and anyone with a heart would certainly not hold that against us.)

Just as the sun was setting, we finally found ourselves home . . . only to discover two of my arch nemesises! (Or is it nemesi? Whatever!) In my absence, two of my enemies had gathered right outside the Petersons' house. Luckily, Justin was nowhere to be seen.

It was the worst thing I'd ever seen. The medusa and a new ice cream monster were preparing to strike at Justin and his family. They were working in tandem now! I had to use my sonic disintegration cone on them all! But just as I was about to charge, I was interrupted.

As both of them came running, the air was filled with the mingling scents of Justin and Phoebe's relief and elation! (By the way, if you've never smelled elation before, it's kind of like movie popcorn and freshly baked chocolate chip cookies.)

I ran and covered Justin in wags and kisses and clicks. Joyously, he clicked back at me and held me in his arms. Mrs. Muffity Puff shared my euphoria and leapt into Phoebe's arms.

"Mrs. Muffity Puff, where have you been?" yelled Phoebe through tears.

"And Sam," said Justin, "where did you go?"

I just looked at Mrs. M, then back to Justin and Phoebe.

"Oh my gosh!" Phoebe said to Justin. "Do you think he ran away to go find her?"

Justin turned back to me. "Is that what you did, Sam? Did you go looking for the cat?"

I answered him with a click.

"Holy smokes, I think you're right! He went out and saved her because he felt guilty."

Finally! These naked-monkey-things were catching on.

"Justin," Phoebe said, turning to him. "I'm sorry for getting mad at you. It wasn't your fault Mrs. Muffity Puff ran away."

"It's okay. I'm sorry we caused so many problems in the first place."

As they made peace, I turned back to my enemies. In this moment of great reunion, I'd completely forgotten we were still standing on a battlefield. And what I saw back at the Peterson place made every hair on my body stand on end.

Gary and Elaine, taking a rare break from their lab, had been beckoned outside by the allure of sweet, sweet ice cream. And they were clearly falling under the spell of the truck's music. But worse than that, they were being flanked by our sworn enemies!

My reunion with Justin would have to wait. I let out my war cry and charged down the hill.

"No, Sam!" yelled Justin, as he chased after me.

I yelled at him to stay back, then I put on the speed and quickly outdistanced him. First stop on the destruction express? Medusa-town!

I charged in, and when she turned to gaze at me, I barked with all my power. But to my surprise, it had no effect. Oh no! The only way to destroy her was to turn her gaze attack on her with a mirror. But where would I ever find a mirror?

Sweet fate had smiled on me! If my sonic bark ray wouldn't work, those mirrors would.

As soon as I had the mirrors in my mouth, I saw the medusa fill with rage. I closed my eyes to avoid her gaze and charged her.

As I circled her and waved the mirrors, I could feel her gaze, but then I knew I'd reflected her evil stare when I saw her fall to the ground with a shriek.

I dropped the mirrors and looked at her as the medusa lay there, defeated. I didn't have time to wait and watch her turn to stone, though. I had to stop *Son of Popsicle Monster* next.

I raced into the crowd. Everyone screamed and scattered except for Elaine and Gary. But amidst the chaos, the Popsicle monster had been separated from the herd. A good thing, because I was about to use my disintegration bark.

Not only had I disintegrated the creature, I had also liberated the last victim that it had eaten, for it spit out the poor soul whole!

Drago and Grisha! Thank goodness! It turned out they were undercover police the entire time. And now they had come to help me fight all these villains!

Oh no! Not Mike! I would have to evade him while I finished off the rest of the Petersons' enemies!

Holy smokes! The pirates had returned too? And they wouldn't be normal pirates anymore, but *zombie* pirates, because certainly they had been bitten by the undead squirrel by now.

Filled with the rush of my many victories, I decided to take the zombie pirates head on.

When I opened my eyes, the pirates and their ship were completely gone. Totally disintegrated!

The sun had set and there was only one remaining Peterson enemy for me to confront: Ghost Wolf.

I ran into the house, followed by my very eager reinforcements. (Well, not exactly. Drago was still game to follow me and fight on, but Grisha lost his nerve and fled. Excusable during such times in battle.)

Victory was at hand as I raced inside the house to find and confront the one enemy I feared most.

Wait, the robot assassin! How could I have forgotten?! If we weren't careful, this thing could easily kill Drago. I aimed my sonic bark disintegrator and let loose on the mechanized horror.

I nailed it! The room was instantly filled with the noxious dust and debris of disintegrated robot!

HA! Like all the others, I smote him, and in his place left nothing but a cloud of ruin.

I knew the way was now safe for Drago, so I pushed forward to the living room, where I hoped my final and most fearsome enemy would be waiting for me.

When I hit the living room, I skidded to a stop and was simultaneously overjoyed and filled with terror that the blinds were open . . .

. . . and there he was, looking just as filled with mixed emotion to see me.

Drago rounded the corner behind me, and the Ghost Wolf—predictably—stole his soul and kept it outside next to him. But simultaneously, Grisha, who must have gained his nerve again, appeared outside behind the Ghost Wolf.

But neither Grisha nor Drago knew that their weapons would have *no effect* on Ghost Wolf. It was up to me.

I ran, barking at Ghost Wolf.

Even as I charged to my potential doom, so too did the Ghost Wolf. I could see Drago and Grisha both aiming their weapons at the creature, but this foe was mine to destroy. Mine and mine alone.

I barked my sonic bark disintegrator at him, and he barked at me, but neither seemed to have any effect as we charged each other. The last thing I remember was my head impacting the head of the Ghost Wolf.

There was a tremendous explosion, and then everything went black. I know now what it feels like to be disintegrated.

Who are you?!

Federal agents, Dr. Peterson.

You didn't want government protection while you worked on your experiment, so we went undercover to keep you safe.

I'm Agent Anita Smith, ma'am, and that dog is a hero. He kept those enemy agents tied up while you finished your work.

ZZ ZZ

211

DAY 20

DEAR DIARY,

Today was the greatest day of my life.

I woke up with a terrible headache, but sweet Justin was there by my side, petting me and hugging me. After a moment, it all came back: how I'd routed our enemies, ending by charging Ghost Wolf and shattering the portal to his evil ghost world.

As I luxuriated in my victory while trying to ignore my aching head, I noticed that my cyber cone was gone. It must've been destroyed when I smashed the ghost portal. Nothing to worry about, though. All of our enemies were vanquished, and . . . well, if that's what it took to drive the

Ghost Wolf away, then so be it.

Phoebe was there too, smiling. Not evil-wizard smiles, either; nice smiles. Mrs. Muffity Puff licked my face as I came to. Thank goodness Phoebe turned out to be a good wizard, or just a normal kid. Either way, clearly she is no threat to Justin or the rest of the family!

Justin called Gary and Elaine to come in as well. I almost didn't recognize them because they weren't scowling and frowning. This time they were actually smiling and happy . . . with me! And their old smells of frustration and anxiety and guilt were totally gone.

"Looks like you're a hero, Sam," said Justin. "Look!"

And with that, he threw a newspaper on the bed.

I still can't read naked-monkey-thing, but there was a picture of Phoebe and Justin in the front yard, smiling. And Phoebe was holding a happy Mrs. Muffity Puff. And there were no villains in the picture at all.

Clearly the newspapers had found out that I'd

emptied the neighborhood of all of its supernatural threats. One quick look out the window at the neighborhood confirmed my hopes: *all* the villains were gone.

Sadly, Drago and Grisha were gone too. I guess after helping me with the monsters, they needed a break, and took that road trip without me. No worries. Next time I saw them, I'd remember to thank them.

Then, sadly, I remembered Meow. Our one great casualty. I was so lost in my thoughts that it seemed as if I could hear the sweet tinkling of his little collar bell in the hall. But then everyone turned away from me, as if they heard the bell too.

And then, to my absolute astonishment, Meow rounded the corner, hopped up on the bed, and covered me in his thick sandpaper kisses. As everyone looked at us, I realized I was not being haunted at all! MEOW WAS ALIVE!!!!

"Meow! You're alive!" I said. "But how??"

"Relax, Sam," said Meow in perfect naked-monkey-thing-ese. "You act like you thought you'd never see me again!"

I could *not* believe my ears. Meow can talk! Did anyone else just hear that?!

"Human–feline gene therapy!" said Elaine.

"We finally did it."

"A perfect DNA splice," added Gary.

"I don't think I'm ever going to get used to a talking cat," Justin said, laughing.

Tears came to my eyes! Not only was he alive, obviously restored to health after the medusa was slain, but now he could talk! *My language lessons had worked!*

Like I said, today was the greatest day of my life. But the best part? Justin and his parents changed my name.

Good boy, Sam, I thought to myself. Now *that's* a name I can be proud of.

ABOUT THE AUTHOR

SAM DAYWALT lives in Southern California with his four naked-monkey-things, two goldfish, a cat, and a lizard named Fritz. Sam's oldest naked-monkey-thing, which he calls "Drew," is the #1 *New York Times* bestselling author of *The Day the Crayons Quit*, *The Legend of Rock Paper Scissors*, and some other books that Sam has forgotten the names of at the moment. Sam spends his time patrolling the grounds of his estate and yelling at the enemy pirate space lords who ring the doorbell disguised as Amazon and UPS delivery drivers

ABOUT THE OTHER GUYS

DREW DAYWALT is the award-winning, *New York Times* bestselling author of *The Day the Crayons Quit* and *The Legend of Rock Paper Scissors*, among many other titles. He lives in Los Angeles with his family and his dog, Sam.

MIKE LOWERY is a *New York Times* bestselling illustrator who has worked on dozens of books for children and adults. He's also the author of many books, including *Random Illustrated Facts* and the Everything Awesome series. He lives in Atlanta, Georgia, with his family.